MW00963198

SUSAN SHREVE

Amy Dunn
QUITS SCHOOL

Pictures by DIANE DE GROAT

TAMBOURINE BOOKS NEW YORK

Text copyright © 1993 by Susan Shreve
Illustrations copyright © 1993 by Diane de Groat

All rights reserved. No part of this book may be reproduced or
utilized in any form or by any means, electronic or mechanical,
including photocopying, recording, or by any information storage
or retrieval system, without permission in writing from the
Publisher. Inquiries should be addressed to
Tambourine Books, a division of William Morrow & Company, Inc.,
1350 Avenue of the Americas, New York, New York 10019.
Printed in the United States of America
Designed by Filomena Tuosto

Library of Congress Cataloging in Publication Data
Shreve, Susan Richards. Amy Dunn quits school/by Susan Shreve;
illustrations by Diane de Groat.—1st ed. p. cm.
Summary: In defiance of her highly attentive mother, who has
filled every moment of her life with plans, schedules, and special
classes, eleven-year-old Amy skips school and goes out
into New York City on her own.
[1. Mothers and daughters—Fiction. 2. New York (N.Y.)—Fiction.]
I. De Groat, Diane, ill. II. Title.
PZ7.S55915Gk 1993 [Fic]—dc20 92-41772 CIP AC
ISBN 0-688-10320-0 (trade)
1 3 5 7 9 10 8 6 4 2
First edition

To E.Q., grown up

CHAPTER 1

Amy woke up early on Halloween, before the sun, her room still dark as night. She got out of bed and turned on the ballerina lamp her mother had gotten her at Bloomingdale's during the years she had wanted Amy to be a ballerina. That was in fourth grade, before her mother had wanted her to be a pianist and the top scholar in the sixth grade at Barton School and the lead in the plays at Levine's School of Drama for Children, where Amy went on Saturdays to study technique with Miss Levine. In the fifth grade, her mother had decided Amy should be a gymnast, since she was small and agile and a quick learner and especially since she had failed ice-skating because she never learned to do twirls or skate backward without falling on her seat. Her mother was thrilled at the beginning of sixth grade when Amy made the A Team in soccer at Barton and would therefore be on the team that played other schools.

"Be a goalie," her mother had said. "You might be able to get a scholarship to college if you're a goalie. I mean, of course, a very good goalie."

Amy was certain that she and her mother were not at all alike, and unlike her mother she had no plans to go to college. In fact, her cousin Cindy, who was spending her life as a waitress in Nantucket and living in a room on the beach with her cat, had told her that at eighteen years old, Amy could pack her suitcase, put away her leotards and soccer balls and books and dancing school dresses forever, and do exactly what she wanted to do every day for the rest of her life.

The trouble was, Amy thought, she had only turned eleven in February, which meant she had seven years to wait.

When she turned on the light, she saw, not to her surprise, the Halloween costume her mother had made her hanging on the outside of the closet—Queen of Hearts with a white satin skirt and a bright-red bodice and puffed sleeves. Her mother must have finished it late last night after their terrible argument about Halloween, after Amy had gone to sleep too upset to complete her composition on friendship for English class.

Nicole Dunn had come home from work at Benson and Jones, where she was a criminal lawyer, at eight o'clock, later than usual, so weary her eyes kept falling closed at the dinner table. They always had dinner together at the round table with a yellow-flowered cloth in the window of the living room that overlooked Eighty-third Street, even when Nicole was late, because she insisted they sit down like an ordinary family and eat dinner.

But they were not an ordinary family. There was only Nicole, who was tall and slender with thick, dark, curly hair, which she wore long like the hair of old-fashioned movie stars whom Amy had read about in magazines. And there was Amy, who was going to be tall, her mother promised, and thin, although for the moment and since she could remember, Amy had been small and round with a soft belly, which stuck out under her belt, and short, black, curly hair. There were no brothers and sisters. No grandparents except her mother's mother, who lived on the desert in Arizona, days from New York. And no father. Amy's father had died before she was born when the motorboat in which he was riding crashed into a dock on Nantucket Island. So as far as Amy knew, in terms of memories, there had never been anyone else in her life but her mother. But Nicole Dunn was enough for any girl to handle, with all her plans for Amy's future.

At the moment, Amy did not like the plans at all. First there was Halloween. Every year the lower school at Barton had a Halloween parade and there was a contest for costumes with prizes for the winners. Every year Nicole decided what Amy should be, made the costume by hand, working late into the night, and every year Amy had come in first or second or third, always winning at least the prize for originality. But sixth grade was the last year in lower school. And in sixth grade most of the girls refused to wear costumes to the Halloween parade. At least, the more grown-up girls.

"I don't want a costume," Amy had said to

her mother in September after her mother had decided that this year it would be Queen of Hearts. "No one in the sixth grade is going to have a costume."

"But, darling," Nicole said, "I talked to Virginia Boyd's mother, and she's having a costume. She's actually renting hers."

"I mean most of the girls," Amy said.

She could not bear to hurt her mother's feelings. After all, her mother did everything for her, anything a daughter could dream of, so much that Amy felt she was going to be smothered with attention, and was afraid she would be dead of suffocation before she was eighteen.

She didn't tell Nicole that Virginia Boyd was a goody-goody and so was everyone else who planned to wear a costume to the Halloween parade.

Now there on the door to her closet was the Queen of Hearts, which her mother had stayed up half the night to finish. Somehow Amy was going to have to figure a way to escape the Halloween parade without making her mother unhappy.

She sat down at her desk and finished her

composition on friendship for Ms. Flye. Then she did four extra credits in math and her science project on photosynthesis, which was not due until the first week in November. Since Barton School started to give letter grades in the fourth grade, Amy had never gotten a grade below an A. Mostly she got A +, except in math which was not her best subject and so she always did the extra credits. Sometimes, she'd lie in bed at night with a terrible feeling in her stomach, her head tight as the skin over a drum, wondering what might happen if the next day a paper in language arts or math or maybe French came back with a B or a C or flunking. What might happen if she flunked? If she, Amy Dunn, number-one student in the sixth grade, got an F? Would she die of it? Would it—and this was her real worry—would it kill her mother?

But most days she didn't have a free minute in her life to worry or even think, because first she had school until three with piano lessons at recess Tuesdays and Thursdays, after which she had soccer practice, and then she took the crosstown bus to French lessons on Tuesday afternoons, the subway to gymnas-

tics on Wednesdays, and on Thursdays, she took a bus up Madison Avenue to ballet, which she especially hated. After spending an hour with a line of skinny ballerinas, looking at themselves in the mirror, she always bought a chocolate ice-cream cone on the way home, sometimes a double dip.

Friday nights were the worst. Friday nights she had dance class in the basement of St. Mark's Episcopal Church, where she was taught to dance with boys who held her back with their sweaty hands, and their breath smelled exactly like sour milk.

"Why?" she had asked her mother about dance class, which had started when she entered the sixth grade. "I HATE boys. I hate to even think there is such a thing as a boy in the same world as I am."

"I know, darling," Nicole had said. "But later, when you're grown up, you'll be glad I made you do this."

"The boys at dancing school carry diseases," Amy said. "I'll probably never grow up from catching their diseases."

But she went to dancing class, of course, just like she did everything else Nicole planned for her life, mostly without an argument, because she was afraid that if she argued, it would upset her mother too much. After all, Nicole had no one else in her life but Amy, and that was a lot of responsibility for an eleven-year-old girl.

Maybe, she thought to herself, listening to her mother on the telephone, making arrangements for a sitter when she went to Washington on business, for a new cleaning lady, for a doctor's appointment for herself, for a dentist's appointment for Amy, organizing, organizing, like a human computer—maybe, Amy was going to be the one to break. Especially if she had to go to Barton that morning on the bus with her Queen of Hearts costume hanging in cellophane and march in the Barton Halloween parade with all the younger students and the goody-goodies in sixth grade. Maybe, she thought to herself, packing up her books for school, making her bed, putting her dirty laundry in the washing machine, she should simply resign this morning after her mother left for work. Call the gymnastics teacher and the piano teacher and the ballet teacher, Miss Levine at Levine's School of Drama for Children, Miss Peachtree at the dancing class in St. Mark's Episcopal Church, and tell them all, she was very sorry to say that she was unable to come to lessons for some time. Perhaps forever. And then she'd call Barton and tell them that her grandmother in Arizona had become ill, and she was leaving immediately for the desert and would be out of school indefinitely. Why not? she thought to herself. That way she wouldn't even have to worry about whether she was Queen of Hearts or not.

She sat down at the breakfast table with her mother. Always, Nicole made a ceremony of things. There were place mats on the table, even at breakfast, cloth napkins, and flowers in a tiny vase in the middle of the table. Together, they would sit side-by-side, making arrangements for the day.

"So this morning, I'll be in court until lunch, and then I have a business lunch with another lawyer, and then in the afternoon, I'll be in my office meeting with a client in case you need me." Nicole always let Amy know exactly where she was in case Amy needed her.

"So this morning, I'll be in math, then spelling, then language arts, then piano at recess, then I have a test in French, then lunch, then history, then math, and at three o'clock, I have soccer."

"Have you given any thought to being goalie?"

"I like playing forward," Amy said. "Coach Jackson says I could get a scholarship to college as a forward," she added to please her mother.

"And is the Halloween parade before soccer?" her mother asked.

"I forgot the Halloween parade," Amy said. "It's at two."

"Well, I should be home by seven, just after you get back from ballet, darling, so we'll have an early dinner since we were up so late last night."

"You were up so late." Amy cleared the table and kissed her mother. "I love the costume."

"Do you love it?" Nicole asked, so pleased that, for a moment, Amy was afraid she could not go on with her plan to resign from the world.

"It's beautiful."

Her mother put on her trench coat, took her

umbrella and briefcase, and kissed Amy good-bye.

"Double lock the door," she called as she always did when she left.

"Bye, Mommy," Amy said. "I will." The front door shut, and Amy was alone in the apartment.

If her mother had said at breakfast that she was planning to come to the Halloween parade because it was Amy's last year in lower school, then things would not have happened as they did. But as it happened, Nicole didn't mention it.

CHAPTER 2

Nicole Dunn punched the down button on the elevator, her head spinning with plans for the day. It was 7:45 A.M. and she was late. It would take her ten minutes to walk to the subway, which, if the trains were running on time, would get her to the office in time to have fifteen minutes to study her notes for the robbery case that was to be tried this morning; then she'd take a taxi to court.

If the trial went according to plans, she would have an hour for lunch with Samuel Godly, and if they finished at one, she would have just enough time to take a cab to Barton School, surprising Amy at the Halloween parade.

Amy did not know that her mother had lunch with Samuel Godly regularly, three times a week. She did not really know Samuel Godly, who was another lawyer in her mother's law firm, although she had met him at the Christmas party at Benson and Jones two years in a row. At the first party Amy told her mother that she had not liked the black-haired man with a dimple called Mr. Godly, who took too much of an interest in her and had asked would she like to meet his son, Christopher.

"Why would I want to meet his son?" Amy had asked crossly on the way home from the Christmas party in a taxi cab. "I have plenty of friends already."

"Mr. Godly was trying to be nice," Nicole had said.

"Well, he was trying too hard," Amy said.

Samuel Godly had been trying very hard to please Nicole Dunn for three years.

"I can't consider actually marrying anyone until Amy graduates from high school," Nicole had said to him. "I am all she has."

"I'm not suggesting that we get married," Samuel Godly said. "I'm just asking you to go out to dinner sometimes, or go to a play or a movie or a trip."

"When Amy is a little older," Nicole had said. "Right now I want to be home for dinner with her."

"I know it's not my business, Nicole," Sam had said. "But you put a lot of pressure on Amy by giving up your whole life for her. Maybe she doesn't want that."

"I really think she expects it," Nicole said.

"Maybe she'd be very pleased to have a night at home without you."

"At the moment, Amy is my whole life," Nicole said quietly.

The truth was, Nicole liked Samuel Godly very much. She would have liked to go out to dinner with him or to a play or even to London as he had asked her to do. She was simply afraid of hurting Amy.

The elevator door opened, and Tyler Brown from the fourteenth floor was there in her lavender running suit with her Lhasa-apso puppy, who was peeing, as usual, on the elevator floor.

"This puppy is driving me crazy," Tyler

said. "I can never make it downstairs in time. Hello, Nicole."

"Hello, Tyler," Nicole said. "Hello, Brie," she said to the puppy.

"You look wiped out," Tyler said. "Were you up all night working?"

"I was up all night making a Halloween costume," Nicole said. "Queen of Hearts."

"Honestly, Nicole, I don't know how you do it. Work and groceries and cooking and Halloween costumes. I'd be in the hospital," she said. "Why didn't you buy a costume? Or rent one? You probably make sugar cookies from scratch. Don't tell me," Tyler raised her hand. "You're an absolutely perfect mother. When Priscilla was Amy's age, I stayed in bed with migraine headaches."

The elevator stopped at the lobby, and Tyler rushed out with Brie.

Nicole walked out the front door into a gray morning with sun like confetti sprinkling the sky.

Tyler was right. She was tired. She would be thirty-four-years old next August, but some days she felt like a very old woman, old enough to be her own grandmother.

She had been twenty the August that she met Amy's father, Peter Dunn, while she was spending her summer on Nantucket Island as a mother's helper for her Aunt Christine's three children. She had been twenty on September 1, 1980, when she and Peter were married in the chapel of the Church of the Heavenly Rest in downtown Albany, New York. And still twenty and pregnant with Amy when he was killed August 11, 1981, in Nantucket. Peter and his little brother Alex had taken an outboard motorboat into the bay so Alex could water-ski.

"Faster, faster," Alex had shouted as they headed in a circle close in to the shore. And Peter looked backward, toward Alex, instead of straight ahead or he would have seen that the boat was headed too close to the dock.

After Peter died, she went back to Albany, New York, where she had grown up and where her family lived. She moved into a small apartment where Amy was born on February 19, 1982—a small, six-pound baby girl with perfectly round eyes and a black cap of curly hair on the top of her head.

When Amy was two, they moved from Albany to New York City so that Nicole could attend Columbia Law School, and they rented the apartment at 495 West End Avenue, Apartment 9B, where they still lived.

From the start, Nicole made up her mind that Amy would have everything a child could wish for—not toys or stereos or two-wheel bicycles—but opportunities to become anything she might wish to become. Amy had dancing lessons and piano lessons and art lessons and French lessons and violin lessons and skating lessons and skiing lessons—everything to make up for the fact that she had no father and no brothers and no sisters and no pets even, because, according to Dr. Delbanco, she was too allergic to cats and dogs and even guinea pigs to have one of them in the apartment.

"I want you to have every opportunity," Nicole told Amy when she was six and started skating lessons at Rockefeller Center. "Who knows? You could turn out to be an Olympic skater."

Nicole put her token in the slot and went through the turnstile. An old man on a bench held out a cup, and she dropped a quarter in. A woman in a purple hat asked her which stop was Lincoln Center and a young girl asked if she had change for the telephone. Nicole leaned against a pillar and closed her eyes. It was 7:55 A.M. Right now Amy Dunn would be putting on her blue-plaid school uniform, her navy-blue tights and Oxford shoes, combing her black curly hair, putting her cereal bowl in the dishwasher, putting on her navy-blue jacket, opening the door to Apartment 9B, pushing the elevator down button, and then seven, which was the floor where her best friend Molly lived, with whom Amy took a bus to school every day since first grade.

The train pulled into the station, and Nicole got on. It was very hard to be everything she had to be—a good mother and a good lawyer and to afford lessons and French tutors and trips to Disneyland and the beach. Some days, like this one, Nicole Dunn simply wanted to move with Amy to a cabin in the woods where there was no school and no law office and no lessons. Only berries to pick for lunch and birds singing in the trees outside their window.

CHAPTER 3

Amy stood next to the front door and listened. She heard the elevator stop on the ninth floor, heard the high-pitched, parrot voice of Tyler, and then her mother's voice, and then they were gone. Then she went to the telephone in the kitchen and called Molly.

"Hello," she whispered to Molly in a low, choked voice. "Guess what?"

"Oh, brother," Molly said. "You're sick. You sound awful."

"I know," Amy said.

She was particularly sorry to tell Molly Loeb a lie, especially since they were best friends. Besides, Nicole had only two rules of conduct and the first was "tell the truth." But Amy needed Molly's help, and she could not very easily tell Molly Loeb—perfect daughter of Eve and Jacob

Loeb, who won the deportment prize at Barton School every year without fail—that she was planning to skip school and spend the day in New York City alone, traveling by subway to Washington Square. Molly was simply not the kind of person to understand skipping school.

"That's terrible, Amy," Molly said, sadly. "You'll miss trick or treat tonight."

"Maybe," Amy said. "But maybe not."

It had not crossed her mind that she'd miss trick or treat. She'd only thought about the Halloween parade.

"If I stay in bed today, I might be fine by tonight."

"I hope so, because Mrs. Gray next door to us has made her apartment into a ghost house again."

"Like last year?"

"Only better."

"Anyway," Amy said, "I won't be going to school today so call me as soon as you get home, and please tell Ms. Cunningham that I'll do my math test on Friday, and tell Ms. Flye that I finished my composition and will bring it in, and tell Sally I'm really sorry to miss soccer."

"Okay," Molly said.

"You didn't change your mind about a costume for today did you?" Amy asked.

"Of course not. We're too old for the Halloween parade, but I'm probably going to wear my father's tuxedo for trick or treat tonight."

"Maybe I'll wear something of my mother's if I'm better, so I'll see you later."

She hung up and dialed Barton School, her heart beating like a drum in her chest. Ms. Applewood, the receptionist, answered the phone.

"Barton School," Ms. Applewood said. "Good morning."

"Good morning, Ms. Applewood," Amy said in her thick voice, full of the sound of illness. "This is Amy Dunn."

"Good morning, Amy. And happy Halloween."

"The same to you," Amy said.

"But you sound as if it's not a very happy Halloween at all."

"Well, no," Amy said. "It's not exactly. I feel terrible, and I'm calling to say that I won't be at school today."

"I'm sorry to hear that Amy," Ms.

Applewood said. "But you know the rules. Your mother has to call to excuse you."

Amy took a deep breath. "My mother would have called," she said. "But she is a criminal lawyer, and this morning she has a very important case to argue at court. So she asked me to call."

"Then you'll remember to have her send me a note tomorrow."

"Of course," Amy said, already thinking that she could type the note on her mother's stationery and copy her mother's signature almost perfectly.

"And I'm so sorry you are missing the Barton parade," Ms. Applewood said. "You always have the best costumes."

"I know," Amy said. "My mother makes them."

"And did she make one this year?"

"Queen of Hearts," Amy said.

Suddenly, it made her very sad to think of her sweet mother up all night, sewing her Queen of Hearts costume. But it was too late to change her mind now. She said good-bye to Ms. Applewood and dialed the Park Avenue School of Ballet.

If there was any part of her week that gave Amy Dunn butterflies in her stomach, it was Thursdays when she took ballet from Mme. Periot.

"First po-si-tion," Mme. Periot would screech. "Amy, Amy. Your stomach is falling on the floor. Hold it in so it's flat as paper."

"My stomach is just like this," Amy would say, crossly.

"No no no no no," Mme. Periot would say. "You can improve." And she'd swoop over Amy. "Tighten like a drum," she'd say pressing the flesh on Amy's stomach. "Pull, pull, pull," and she'd turn Amy's feet straight out in first position.

"I really wanted to be a dancer when I was your age," Nicole Dunn had said. "I daydreamed of sailing across the stage on toe. But my mother said, 'Absolutely no. Ballet is for floozies.' "

"What is a floozy?" Amy had asked.

"I never asked," Nicole said, sadly.

Amy did not bother to tell her mother that she had never in her life daydreamed of being a ballerina and certainly never would.

*   *   *

Mme. Periot answered the phone after the second ring.

" 'Allo, 'allo, 'allo," she said. "Yes, Amy. I am so sorry you have a sickness but as soon as you are well, you must practice with that flopping stomach of yours, if you want to be in *The Nutcracker* this Christmas."

"I don't want to be in *The Nutcracker*, of course," Amy thought but she only said of course and good-bye to Mme. Periot.

She hung up the phone, and then she dialed Mr. Barnes who taught her piano at Barton during recess. Mr. Barnes never answered the telephone. He sat all day in his apartment when he was not teaching and practiced the piano. If the telephone rang, he stopped playing long enough to listen to the message, and then he played on. So when his answering machine came on, Amy said, "This is Amy Dunn, and I will not be at piano today because as you can hear, I am too sick."

When she finished her last telephone call, it was 8:15, and she settled in front of the television to watch cartoons until all of the people at 495 West End Avenue had left for school and work so she would not be caught. Two telephone calls came, which she did not answer, but the answering machine was on so she listened to the messages. The first was from Pest Control, saying he would be spraying for German roaches on Friday morning between seven and seven-thirty. The second was from Mme. Periot. "Mrs. Dunn," she said in her high voice. "This is Mme. Periot calling. I know today that Amy is too ill to come for ballet, but please telephone me so we can discuss her progress, which is not so good." Amy waited for the machine to click off, and then she erased the message from Mme. Periot. Perhaps, she thought, she ought to turn the answering machine off just in case Barton School called or Mr. Barnes rang about piano.

At nine o'clock, she turned off the television and went into her mother's room, looking through the drawers of her bureau. Not that Nicole would have minded exactly. "Everything of mine is yours, darling," she had said to Amy.

That was the trouble. Nicole tried so hard to be the perfect mother that Amy always worried about hurting her feelings. Sometimes she wished her mother were less generous, less agreeable, more like the mothers of her friends—like Molly's mother, Eve, who had a bad temper and had said just last Friday and in Amy's presence, "My room is my room and you stay out of it, Molly Loeb."

The top drawer of Nicole's dresser had papers mostly, letters and photographs, most of which Amy had seen before. But in the middle of a stack of letters was a picture of her father that she did not remember, a full-length picture of a young and handsome man in a sailor cap and shorts, standing on the bow of a sailboat, holding the mast with one hand. *For Nicole, Love of my Life, Forever, Peter. Nantucket, 1981.* Amy had seen a few pictures of her father, not many: pictures of their wedding in Albany, New York; a serious picture of her father in a suit and tie, which sat on a table in the living room in a silver frame. But she had never seen a picture taken the summer of 1981 when he died, the summer he knew that he was going to have a baby, although he did not know that she would turn out to be a girl called Amy Nicole Dunn. This picture was different than other pictures she

had seen. In this picture, Peter Dunn seemed to be the sort of man she would like to have as a father, the sort of man who might have made her mother less serious and hard working than she was. She closed her mother's bureau drawer and took the picture to her own room, hiding it underneath her sweaters in her bottom drawer.

Then she looked in her closet and closed the door. She did not want to wear her own clothes today. In the full-length mirror on her door, she looked like a short, plump, curly-haired girl, closer to eight-years old than eleven. That was not the look she wanted for her day of freedom in New York City. In her mother's closet, she checked through the long skirts and trousers and came upon a wrap-around skirt that fit around her waist and a long, brown, turtleneck sweater. The skirt was too long, but she rolled it up, and the sweater was square and fit over the waistband. In the bathroom, she put on her mother's powder, rose blush on her plump cheeks, black mascara, and in the long mirror on the door, she looked quite grown up.

The telephone rang, and it was Ms. Applewood talking on the machine. "Oh, Amy," she said in her high-flying voice. "I thought you would be answering the phone but you are probably sleeping. This message is for Ms. Dunn, just to remind you to send a note with Amy about her absence today. Have a good day."

Amy erased the message, turned on the dishwasher, turned off the bathroom light, and just before she left the apartment, she went into her bedroom, opened the door where her Queen of Hearts dress was hanging, took the material in her arms, and kissed the costume. "I am so sorry not to wear you today," she said with a sharp feeling of sorrow for her mother's hard work.

The clock on the hall table read nine-thirty, which gave her just enough time to get to Washington Square by ten o'clock.

Washington Square, downtown in Greenwich Village, was Amy's favorite place in New York City. But ever since June, when her Mother's purse was stolen in the middle of the day as they watched a juggler on the northwest corner of the park, Nicole had refused to take Amy there.

CHAPTER 4

Nicole Dunn sat down at the desk in her small office overlooking Forty-fifth Street and checked her TO DO list for Thursday, October 31.

1. Dentist appointment for Amy.
2. Call Mme. Periot about the schedule for *The Nutcracker.*
3. Call Barton to arrange for Amy to take ice-skating during the winter term.
4. Buy new underclothes.
5. Buy vitamin pills.
6. Get tickets for the ballet on Saturday and ask Molly if she'd like to come.
7. Ask Dr. Delbanco about the mole on Amy's forehead.

She pushed the list aside and opened her notes for the robbery of Larkins Fine Jewelry on Fifth Avenue that had taken place on April 11, 1991, at four in the afternoon, when Bruce Tarking of 11 East Fifty-second Street had entered the jewelry store with a black plastic gun from the toy department at Macy's and robbed the Larkins Fine Jewelry store of four thousand dollars' worth of diamond and emerald and ruby rings. He had put the jewelry in his book bag, with his schoolbooks, left the store, and according to Mr. Larkin, who called the police, Bruce Tarking had turned left toward Fiftieth Street and disappeared in the crowd. What Bruce Tarking, age fourteen and a half, had actually done, according to his testimony to the police, was to get on the crosstown bus, get off across the street from his apartment, go into his building, up the elevator to the fourth floor, let himself in the door, go to his room, and hide the jewelry underneath the bed in an old toy box where he kept his sports equipment for gym. By the next morning, the police had a positive identification of Bruce Tarking, and by that afternoon, the Tarkings had called the offices of Benson and Jones, specialist in juvenile crimes, and Nicole Dunn had been assigned to the case. It was an unusual case for Nicole Dunn because Bruce Tarking was an ordinary boy, without a criminal record. He was a fair student, a good athlete at PS 107, and had just read the story of *Robin Hood* for a book report. As a result of reading Robin Hood's adventures, he decided to steal a toy gun from Macy's, rob a jewelry store, sell the jewelry to a pawnshop as he had seen done on television, and distribute the money to the poor homeless men and women who lined the doorways and alleys along First Avenue.

"The trouble is," as Nicole told Amy, with whom she discussed her cases over dinner. "He is guilty of the crime of which he is accused, so he will have to be punished. But from the point of view of a young boy, his reasons for stealing were admirable."

"That's why I don't think he should be punished," Amy had said.

"But under the law, you are judged for what you have done," Nicole had said. "Not what you intend to do."

"That's unfair," Amy had said in a temper.

"Like ballet. I can't do what I intend to do, so Mme. Periot screams at me."

"That's not exactly the same thing," Nicole had said reasonably.

"Sometimes I hate that you're a lawyer and always so sensible and serious," Amy said and left the table without touching her dinner.

That night Nicole could not sleep. It had never occurred to her that Amy did not like ballet. Maybe her daughter was not as cheerful as she seemed. Maybe Nicole had misjudged her. Sometime soon she should talk to Amy about her activities and her schoolwork and her athletics to be sure she was happy.

The telephone rang in her office and it was Sam Godly.

"Lunch at the Austin Grille," he asked. "I've ordered a table by the window."

"I have to make it at twelve o'clock today, Sam," Nicole said. "It's the Barton School Halloween parade, and I want to be there on time."

"Isn't Amy getting a little old for Halloween parades?" he asked.

"Not at all," Nicole said, a little crossly. "She's only in the sixth grade."

"Well, twelve o'clock is fine, but I may be a few minutes late. Good luck on your argument today."

Nicole gathered her papers on the desk and put them in her briefcase. She took her umbrella just in case, put on blush and pale lipstick, brushed her hair, and closed the door to her office.

Her secretary, Victoria, who sat just outside Nicole's office, was hanging up the telephone.

"Good morning, Victoria," Nicole said, dropping a list of things to do on Victoria's desk.

"Hi, Nicole," Victoria said. "I was just talking to Amy's ballet teacher."

"Mme. Periot?"

"I told her you'd call her back later," Victoria said. "And she said she hoped Amy felt better."

"Amy's fine," Nicole said. "I wonder why she said that." She shrugged. "I won't be back in the office until about four-thirty, because I have Amy's Halloween parade after lunch."

"And lunch with Sam at the Grille?"

"That's right."

"Well, good luck with your case today." Victoria waved.

"Thank you, Victoria," Nicole said and she went down the elevator, through the lobby, and out into the soft light of morning on Fifth Avenue at Forty-fifth Street to hail a taxicab.

CHAPTER 5

When Amy left the apartment with her backpack, money she had taken from the emergency money jar in the linen closet, and an umbrella just in case of rain, Mr. Rappaport from Apartment 9C was waiting for the elevator.

"Hello, Mr. Rappaport," Amy said, standing next to him with her head bowed, so he would not notice the rose makeup or the mascara.

"Call me Guy," Mr. Rappaport said. He always said, "Call me Guy," but Amy never did. It was always "Mr. Rappaport" and "How is your painting, Mr. Rappaport?" since Mr. Rappaport spent the days in his apartment painting in oil very small miniatures of circuses, which people could buy at a gallery in the Village for quite a lot of money.

"And what are you doing at nine-thirty on Halloween morning?" he asked. "Did you get the day off?"

"Not exactly," Amy said, thinking what excuse could she give to Mr. Rappaport, wondering how she could slip away from him. "I have a dentist's appointment."

"Ahh, the dentist," Mr. Rappaport said. "Look." He bent down and pulled at his upper teeth, which came out in his hand, making Amy shriek, which seemed to please him. "Store-bought teeth. So I don't ever have to go to the dentist."

The elevator stopped at the lobby and they walked out of the building together towards Eighty-sixth Street and the subway.

"Where are you going?" Amy asked.

"With you," Mr. Rappaport said.

"I mean really," Amy said.

"That's what I mean too," Mr. Rappaport said. "I got up this morning, had a bagel and orange juice, fed my canary, and realized I was not interested in painting today, so I decided I'd just leave the apartment and see what came up," he said, patting Amy on the top of her black curls. "And you came up."

Oh, brother, Amy thought as they stood at Eighty-sixth Street, waiting to cross West End Avenue. It was her first and maybe only day of freedom in her whole life. Now it was likely that Guy Rappaport from Apartment 9C was going to ruin it.

Amy actually liked Guy Rappaport. Unlike most of the people who lived at 495 West End Avenue, he was never in a hurry. In fact there was even a time, when she was quite a lot younger and daydreamed about fathers, that she used to pretend Mr. Rappaport married Nicole, and they moved to a very large apartment across from Central Park, and her mother stayed home all day baking cakes for Amy and Mr. Rappaport.

"Mr. Rappaport?" Nicole laughed when Amy told her. "If I ever get married again, which I probably won't, it certainly won't be to Mr. Rappaport."

Amy often imagined fathers for herself and husbands for Nicole. Sometimes she imagined the fathers of her friends or teachers at Barton School or even the men she saw in

magazines. Especially lately. Lately, whenever she was with Molly and her father or her friend Terry's father or Camilla's father, she longed to have a father of her own.

But looking now at Mr. Rappaport with black, fuzzy curls on the back of his neck and a plump, gray beard around his chin, she could understand why her mother had not been interested in marrying him.

The morning was warm for late October and sunny, a perfect day for the Halloween parade at Barton School, Amy thought, walking down the long dark steps into the subway station, Mr. Rappaport chattering beside her.

"If you'd like me to wait at the dentist's office, I'll walk you to school afterward."

Amy put her token in the slot and walked through the turnstile toward the downtown trains.

"Or we could stop and have a Coke," Mr. Rappaport was saying but the train hurtled into the station then and Amy could not hear him.

She sat down next to a boy in a wooly cap with a headset on, dancing to music with his feet, and Mr. Rappaport took hold of the rail beside her. She had to think quickly, or else she would have to tell Mr. Rappaport the truth that she was not going to the dentist's and instead was spending the day at Washington Square.

If she were with her mother, Nicole would insist on an educational morning at the Museum of Natural History or the Museum of Modern Art or even the zoo. But what Amy really wanted to do was to get off the subway, walk to Washington Square, sit on a park bench next to one of the old bag ladies, half sleeping in the sun, and watch the jugglers and roller bladers and rap singers shouting their furies to the world, the magicians performing for the tourists, and the chess players and street preachers and the drunk old ladies singing their sad stories. Then she would go to the ice-cream shop on Waverly Place and order a double-dip sundae with hot fudge and whipped cream. But if Mr. Guy Rappaport didn't disappear pretty soon, she was going to have to think of another plan.

Mr. Rappaport was speaking to her, but she kept her head down and pretended not to hear him. He leaned over and whispered in her ear.

"Where is your dentist's office?" he asked.

She looked up, shaking her head.

"Your dentist's office?" he asked.

Perhaps if she sat very still and concentrated on the people's feet across from her in the subway, then Mr. Rappaport would leave her alone. But at Fifty-ninth Street, the boy in the headphones got off, and Mr. Rappaport sat down next to her.

"So," he said, pleased with himself. "Where do we get off?"

"Washington Square is where I get off," Amy said quietly.

"Great," Mr. Rappaport said. "I love Washington Square. My favorite is the sword swallower." He dipped his head back and pretended to swallow an imaginary sword. "Have you seen the sword swallower?"

Amy shook her head.

"He's amazing," he said. "I can't even swallow a whole green bean."

When the train stopped at Forty-second Street, the woman seated next to Mr. Rappaport, a pretty woman in a bright green hat, tapped him on the arm. "Aren't you Guy Rappaport?" she asked.

"I am indeed," he said.

"Well, I'm Paula True, and we went to PS 109 together," she said.

"I remember you exactly, Paula True," Mr. Rappaport said happily.

At the Thirty-fourth Street stop, they were still talking, and at Twenty-third Street, Mr. Rappaport was laughing loud enough for the elderly man in the seat across from Amy to say, "Pipe down!" At Fourteenth Street, Paula True stood up, and Guy Rappaport followed her right off the subway, waving to Amy. "Have a nice dentist's appointment," he called. "See you in the elevator."

And Amy was alone.

At Greenwich Village, she got off the subway, and went up the steps into a bright clear morning. On the corner of the street, a vendor was selling cotton candy, pink and purple mix, and Amy bought one, walked across the street into the Square, taking a seat on a park bench next to a woman in a heavy winter coat and hiking boots and a green garbage bag tied on top of her head with a ribbon, as if she were expecting rain.

"I haven't eaten in two weeks," the woman,

who was eating a Mars bar, said to Amy. "Could you spare a quarter?"

Amy reached in her blazer pocket and took out a quarter.

"I want two quarters," the woman said crossly. "You can't buy anything with one quarter."

If Nicole had been there, she would have taken Amy by the hand and marched across the park and hailed a taxi. Nicole didn't like trouble of any kind. But Amy reached into her pocket and gave the woman another quarter.

The woman grunted.

"You ought to at least say thank you," Amy said.

"Thank you," the woman said.

Two young boys on skateboards flew past Amy and jumped off.

"Hey, girlie," one of them, not much older than Amy, said. "You busy?"

Amy didn't reply.

The other boy reached over, pulled off a bit of her cotton candy, and stuck it in his mouth.

"Not bad," he said. "Try it, dude," he said to his friend.

The friend reached over and started to take some of the cotton candy, but as he did, the woman in the garbage bag hit him across the arm with her umbrella.

"You leave us alone," she said.

"Sure, grandma," the boy called Dude said, hopping back on his skateboard, his friend following. "I didn't know you were related." And they sailed across the park.

"Thank you," Amy said.

The woman smiled, pleased with herself. "Have you got another quarter for a pack of cigarettes?" she asked.

"I thought you wanted to eat."

"Nope," the woman said. "Now I want a smoke."

"I haven't got another quarter," Amy said. "But you can finish this." She handed the woman the rest of her cotton candy, got up, and walked across the park to the center where she had seen a juggler in costume.

It was peculiar to be absolutely alone, a stranger to everyone she saw except herself. And Amy Dunn felt wonderful. Nothing much had happened, but she had, on her own with-out her mother or Molly Loeb or Terry or Camilla, made friends with a woman in a garbage bag, who had protected her against two, maybe, dangerous boys. The world around her seemed much grander and more exciting than it had ever seemed sitting, as she ought to have been, in Ms. Cunningham's math class, doing her unit test on fractions.

When she sat down on a park bench surrounded by enthusiastic pigeons, the juggler had no audience.

"See, sweetheart," the juggler said to her, tossing first yellow and then blue balls in the air. "For you, I do these pretty colored balls," he said. Then he tossed apples. "And just for you, I do apples." He tossed Amy an apple, and she caught it. "A little lunch for the lady," he said. "And now for you, my best customer on this Halloween day, I do my most dangerous trick." He held a long knife up in the air. And then a second. "Knives for the lady," he sang, tossing them in the air, beginning to dance, twirling them so they spun, handle first, into his hand. "Hop-a-long Cassidy, whoopee," he sang, the knives twirling round and round, flying in the air. "Come along, baby, and dance with me."

Amy took two quarters out of her pocket and tossed them in the box in front of the juggler.

"Fifty cents, darling. Only fifty cents when I am doing my knives for you personally?"

Amy reached into her pocket and took out a dollar, which she dropped in the box. But the juggler was making her uneasy. She was beginning to wish she had stayed with Mr. Rappaport and was just about to leave, when the two skateboarders flew across the park in her direction and stopped short right next to Amy Dunn.

CHAPTER 6

At eleven-thirty, Nicole Dunn finished at court and took a taxi to the Austin Grille.

The Austin Grille was a small restaurant on Waverly Place where Nicole came with Amy once a month, sometimes more. Always they ordered shrimp in garlic sauce, lemon cake, and cappucino, which was Nicole's favorite choice of dinners. The first time Amy had been old enough to order for herself, she ordered the same thing.

"Are you sure?" Nicole had asked. "This is not a little girl's kind of dinner."

"Since you like it," Amy had said with confidence, "I will too."

Which was the way Amy had always felt about everything Nicole chose, until recently.

When they went to dinner at the Austin Grille, Nicole gave Amy a sip of her wine, and they leaned over the white-clothed table and told secrets. Then they walked down Waverly Place holding hands.

It was Nicole's favorite time with Amy, although she tried to do important and educational things with her too—the Museum of Natural History or the Museum of Modern Art, or the programs at the zoo, sometimes an off-Broadway play or a play at the Public Theatre. But the weekends she really looked forward to were the ones, especially in winter, when they walked all the way downtown on Saturday, stopping for ice cream at Washington Square, going to a movie at the theatre on West Eleventh, and then wandering to Waverly Place for dinner at the Austin Grille.

Nicole was early. And very tired. She sat down at a table next to a window, which was open onto the warm sunny afternoon, ordered a diet Coke, took off her shoes, and put her feet up on the chair across from her. It was noon. Amy was probably at lunch. And after lunch, there would be a Halloween party in the cafeteria and then they'd put on their costumes for the parade. She had forgotten to tell Amy to borrow some makeup, particularly lipstick. She hoped Amy had not outgrown her white shoes from last summer.

Samuel Godly was late. She checked her watch. Sam Godly was very seldom late. She liked that about him. She liked the fact that she could depend on him and that he made her laugh. Sometimes she was lonely for people her own age, and Sam Godly was her age, thirty-three this year. He lived alone in an apartment on West Twenty-ninth and on weekends his son, Christopher, a little younger than Amy, came to visit him from Long Island where he lived with his mother. On weekends, when she and Amy visited the museums or window shopped on Madison Avenue or went skating at Rockefeller Plaza, Nicole daydreamed of meeting Sam Godly with Christopher. All four of them could have dinner together and afterward, she daydreamed that Amy might say to her, "I really liked that man and his son, Christopher. We should go out together again."

But the truth was, they had never run into

Sam and Christopher on their Saturday out-
ings in the city.

She was resting her chin on her elbows,
almost asleep, when Sam sat down, gave a
little pull on her curly bangs, and kissed her
on the cheek.

"You look like you're ready for bed," he said,
removing her feet from the chair.

"I was up all night making Amy's costume,"
Nicole said. "She's Queen of Hearts."

"I'm sure it's a beauty," Sam said, looking
at the menu. "But you really do too much for
her, Nicole."

"Please, Sam," Nicole said.

"I'm not trying to criticize you," he said,
ordering two Salade Nicoise, as usual, and
lemonade for him. "I worry about Amy. She
has so much to do every day, that some morn-
ings she must get up and think, today I'd like
to lie around and eat popcorn and watch TV
and stay in my pajamas."

Nicole laughed. "Me too," she said.

"Well, you guys ought to try it," Sam said.
"Just a whole day with popcorn and TV." He
took out a notebook from his jacket pocket.
"Here are your messages from Victoria. You

have an appointment at five-thirty with a guy named Mr. Sanborn and a breakfast meeting tomorrow morning at seven-thirty with a new client and Amy's piano teacher called about her missing piano today."

"Missing piano?" Nicole asked. "I don't think she is missing piano." She put the pink slip with her messages in her purse. "Unless the Halloween parade is interfering with her piano lesson."

She ordered berries for dessert and a cup of coffee.

"So," she said. "What are you doing this weekend?"

"I was going to talk to you about that," Sam said. "Christopher will be visiting on Saturday, and he has never been to the Statue of Liberty."

"Nor have I," Nicole said. "It's so odd to have lived in New York for nine years and not to have been there."

"Good. Because I wonder if you and Amy would like to come with us, and then we could have dinner later—maybe here."

"Well," Nicole shrugged. "I'll ask Amy."

"She'll love it. I promise."

Nicole smiled.

"Maybe," she said. She checked her watch, and it was almost one-thirty. "I'll ask her and tell you tomorrow," she said.

"Wait," Sam said, paying the bill. "I'll leave with you. I've got an appointment."

They walked out of the restaurant to Waverly Place. As usual, Sam kissed her on the cheek.

"See you later," he said.

Nicole hailed a cab. "The Barton School," she said, "Seventy-second and Lexington." She settled into the backseat.

She would ask Amy tonight about the Statue of Liberty. Maybe—just maybe, they would all have a good time.

CHAPTER 7

Amy was still sitting on the bench in front of the juggler, when the skateboard boys stopped right in front of her.

"So what are you going to do now?" the boy called Dude said.

"I'm going to school," Amy said, her heart picking up a beat in her chest.

"To school?" the other boy said, taking her by the shoulders. "What's a girl like you doing going to school?"

Amy stood up to leave but he held her tight.

"I go to school, of course," Amy said, and feeling the need for protection from these boys, she added, "And now, I'm meeting my father, who is right over there."

Amy scanned the Square for a man, any man, in the distance, whom she could pretend was her father. *Yea!* she thought. Walking toward them, quite far away, the length of a soccer field at least, was a man. She couldn't tell what kind of man—whether he was old or young or dressed in a business suit or jeans or the loose, tattered clothes of the bums so often seen wandering through Washington Square. But she knew he was a man, so she pulled her shoulders loose from the boy called Dude and pointed in his direction.

"There," she said. "That's my father."

The boys looked down the walk under the spread of red and golden yellow oak trees.

"That's your father?"

"Yes," Amy said, folding her arms across her chest, ready for a chance to run. The boys stood side by side, one foot on their skateboards. The one called Dude reached into the pocket of his jeans and pulled out a Tootsie Roll Lollipop, sticking it in his mouth.

In the corner of her eye, Amy saw the juggler tossing the blue and yellow balls in the air.

"Maybe you ought to ask your Papa for five bills," the juggler said in a singsong voice. "Tell him I did the knives special for you."

Amy slipped by Dude and his friend and walked straight in the direction of the man she had identified as her father. She did not want to run now, since certainly they were faster than she was, even without their skateboards.

"I will ask him about five dollars," Amy called over her shoulder to the juggler.

She could feel the presence of the boys behind her, standing, she guessed, exactly as she had left them, watching her. She could hear the slap of the balls against the juggler's palm and he was singing: "I got yellow and blue balls, orange and red and green balls, purple and plum balls, flying in the air."

But she felt quite safe in the bright sunlight and proud of herself, proud of her independence, walking toward her imaginary father.

As she got closer to the man, not close enough to see his face, but close enough to see that he was not well dressed—that he was young but walking very slowly as if he were in fact an old man with a bad leg—she could tell he was swaying. With every step or two, he seemed to stumble to the right. She did not look behind her to see if the boys were still there, but she assumed they were. And when she was close enough to see the man's face, a berry-brown face whose features were disguised by a square beard and a long mustache above his upper lip, she knew that he had been drinking. A strange smile crossed his face.

"Hello, sweetheart," he said to her quietly as she came upon him. "You wouldn't happen to have a dollar for a cup of coffee?"

Amy reached in her pocket and took out the small wad of bills she had taken from the emergency money jar, unfolding them, giving him a dollar. Behind her, she saw the boys still standing there and the juggler with his hands on his hips.

The man took her dollar and wandered on and then Amy ran, dashing across the street when the light turned green, and into Maureen's Sweet and Sundae Shop, taking a seat in the back, facing the door, just in case the boys had seen her and followed her to Maureen's.

The waitress handed her a menu.

"Are you alone?" she asked.

Amy nodded. "I want a double-dip sundae with one chocolate, and one mint chocolate chip with hot fudge and lots of whipped cream," she said a little out of breath.

So, that was easy, she thought, very pleased with herself for escaping Dude and his friend—although she guessed they probably were not particularly dangerous. Only troublesome. But she was glad that she had gotten away so easily, that she had survived Washington Square, that they had believed her story about her father.

For a girl who almost never lied, Amy Dunn was having a very strange day.

She checked her watch. It was one o'clock. At school, her class had finished lunch and were either in the gym or in the library returning their books for the week. The picture of her Queen of Hearts costume hanging on the back of her closet in its cellophane bag slid across her mind, and she wondered suddenly if there were any chance that her mother might decide to go to the parade. Usually Nicole was dependable about her plans for the day and did not surprise Amy. But today, since it was the last Halloween parade of Amy Dunn's life, maybe her mother had changed her mind, she thought, eating the sundae slowly, piles of soft, sweet cream and hot chocolate slipping across her tongue. But probably not.

It was quarter of two when Amy left Maureen's Sweet and Sundae Shop, round-bellied with ice cream. Maybe she'd walk home, all the way uptown, she thought, and then she could take the crosstown bus at Eighty-sixth. If she walked slowly, stopping at FAO Schwartz Toy Store to look around, and maybe the Gap, she would be home just about the time Molly Loeb arrived from school. And when Molly called, she would say she was better than she had been in the morning, well enough for trick-or-treating before supper.

She walked along Waverly Place, past the brownstone where her mother's cousin lived, past Koala Blue where Nicole had bought a new jacket and a pair of jeans last week, past the small gallery where Mr. Rappaport's paintings of circuses were for sale. Amy looked through the window and saw a neat display of several small paintings, lined up perfectly across the wall. From where she was standing, she could see the tiny elephants and tigers with acrobats standing in various positions on their backs. Up close, she knew that all of the miniature animals and people had carefully drawn features, sprinkles of freckles across their noses, frowns on their foreheads, tiny birthmarks on their cheeks. Once, in the years that Amy had daydreamed of her mother marrying Guy Rappaport, Mr. Rappaport had given her one of his paintings, called *Circus Performers at Lunch*, which showed two acrobats, a man and a woman, in lavender leotards and turquoise-blue tops, eating their small lunch of turkey sandwiches, sitting on the back of an elephant. Amy particularly liked the detail of the sandwiches with a miniature tomato and a slip of lettuce showing between the slices of bread.

She crossed the street, walking a familiar route she often walked with Nicole, up Wa-

verly Place toward the Austin Grille. Just as she started up Waverly, she caught sight of a woman who looked very much like Nicole, dressed as her mother had been dressed that morning in a navy-blue skirt and jacket, with a wide, brightly colored scarf around her neck. *Could it actually be my mother?* Amy thought. And she knew it was her mother, coming out of the Austin Grille with a man exactly her height. Nicole put her hand on the man's arm, just above the elbow, and he kissed her.

The breath went out of Amy Dunn. She ducked into the doorway of Sansar Interiors, leaned against the wall so she would not be seen, her eyes closed, her legs shaking. But by the time she looked again, her mother and the man were gone.

CHAPTER 8

Nicole was late for the Barton School Halloween parade. She ran up the steps, past the lines of children in costume waiting to march across the stage, and slid into an aisle seat in the back of the auditorium packed with children and parents. The piano was playing "Puff the Magic Dragon" when she arrived, and the children had started their colorful parade, down the center aisle and up the steps to the stage where the judges sat in hard back chairs facing the audience. There were fairies and rabbits and witches and baseball players, Batman and televisions and queens and Olympic gold medalists. There was a large black bear and a ballet dancer and a cat with whiskers that hung to the floor, a birthday present wrapped in red ribbon, Robin Hood and Wendy from *Peter Pan* and Peter Pan himself and Captain Hook.

Nicole settled back into her seat and waited for the older children, last in line, to parade into the auditorium.

Molly Loeb, without a costume, came in with Camilla and Beatrice and Cheryl, but Amy was not among them. Nicole gave a little wave to Molly as she walked by.

"I didn't know you were coming," Molly said.

"Surprise." Nicole smiled.

"Surprise?" The look on Molly's face was bewildered.

"That's right," Nicole said. "Surprise."

Molly Loeb leaned over when she sat down and whispered in Camilla's ear. For a moment, Nicole was uncomfortable that she had made a costume for Amy this year, since her friends were in the audience without costumes. After all, Amy had said herself in early September that she did not want a costume, that she did not really want to march in the Halloween parade. The well-liked, regular, popular sixth graders would not be marching, she had said. But by the next day, she had changed her mind. Of course, she had said, she would love to be Queen of Hearts. She had been "just kidding" about the parade.

Perhaps, Nicole thought, *she had not been "just kidding" at all.* Nicole folded her hands in her lap and waited—through the boy in the tuxedo and the girl in her mother's wedding dress and the girl, maybe it was Sarah Ponds, dressed as Madonna, and the boy as a telephone with a long wire attached to a very tall girl in a body stocking. There was a girl dressed as the principal of Barton School and a Lady Macbeth and a Pinocchio. Nicole waited as each member of the sixth-grade class who had chosen to wear a costume passed across the stage in front of the judges.

And there was no Amy Dunn. No Queen of Hearts.

Maybe, at the last minute, Amy had changed her mind. Maybe, at this very moment, she was in the girls' bathroom on the first floor, getting out of her costume, embarrassed not to be sitting in the auditorium next to Molly Loeb and Camilla.

Molly turned around in her seat, four rows to the right, and Nicole caught Molly's eye, raising her hands in a gesture of question. "Where is Amy?" she mouthed. Molly shook her head and leaned over to whisper in Camilla's ear. The prizes were announced for Best All-Around Costume, the Grand Prize which Amy usually won, and for most original and prettiest and funniest, to the cat with long whiskers and the black bear and the telephone, but Nicole was too worried to listen. Where could Amy be? Why hadn't anyone mentioned anything to her about her daughter? Was she possibly sick in the infirmary? Had she fallen in gym? She looked around at the sea of faces in the auditorium, but no Amy. She waited until the recession, the children marching to Sousa's band music, and then she got up, smiling at the principal, shaking hands with Ms. Landon, Amy's fourth grade teacher, passing through the auditorium doors into the hallway.

She had to find Ms. Applewood. Ms. Applewood knew everything about the comings and goings of the children. Surely she would know where Amy had been during the Halloween parade.

But when Nicole got to reception, Ms. Applewood was not at her desk. Another woman, answering the telephones, looked up when Nicole walked in.

"May I help you?" She smiled.

"I'm looking for Ms. Applewood."

"Ms. Applewood had an appointment at three o'clock so I'm taking her place," she said. "I'm Alice Little's mother."

"Oh, hello," Nicole said, hoping that her voice was not shaking. "I'm Amy Dunn's mother, Nicole, and I'm looking for my daughter, who is in the sixth grade."

"Was she in the Halloween parade? A few of the sixth graders came in costume."

"She had a costume," Nicole said. "Queen of Hearts. But," and she shrugged, "I didn't see her in the parade."

"Let me check the sixth-grade office." Alice Little's mother picked up the telephone. "What homeroom is she in?"

"Ms. Barker's."

"Ms. Barker?" she said speaking into the

receiver. "Ms. Dunn is here looking for Amy." She paused and looked through some papers on her desk. "Oh, I see," she said. "Yes. I see her name on the list. Yes. Of course." She hung up the phone.

"Ms. Dunn," Alice Little's mother said in a soft, kind voice reserved for bad news. "Amy didn't come to school today."

"She didn't come to school today?" Nicole repeated, her heart beating in her throat.

Alice Little's mother showed Nicole the list of absentees.

"She was ready for school when I left for work this morning," Nicole said, trying to calm her voice, to speak slowly and without trembling. "She had a costume, Queen of Hearts," she said. "Oh, I told you that already." She was afraid she was going to cry in front of this stranger. "Could I ask Molly Loeb in sixth grade? Amy rides to school with Molly, who is also in Ms. Barker's class."

"We'll call Ms. Barker back," Alice Little's mother said. She handed Nicole the phone.

"Ms. Barker," Nicole said, her voice full of tears. "This is Nicole Dunn."

"Oh, hello, Ms. Dunn," Ms. Barker said as if nothing in the world were the matter.

"I wonder if I could speak to Molly Loeb," Nicole said.

"Molly has gone with the rest of the girls in the class on the bus for soccer practice," Ms. Barker said.

"Of course, that's where Amy should be. I mean if she were in school, she'd be at soccer," she said nervously. "Thank you, Ms. Barker."

She handed the phone back to Alice Little's mother. "Thank you," she said in a thin voice and left the reception office. She walked down the long corridor, past the library and the gymnasium to the entrance to the Barton School at the corner of Seventy-second and Lexington, where she hailed a taxi.

"Four ninety-five West End Avenue," she said to the driver, her mind flooded with nightmares.

CHAPTER 9

After Nicole disappeared into a taxicab, Amy walked uptown, thinking about the man she had seen with her mother. *It was not an important kiss between them*, she thought. Not like the kisses she had seen at the movies. The man could be a friend, another lawyer in her mother's office, even a client who was more friendly than most. But he could just possibly be her mother's boyfriend. Which meant her mother had a secret from her, Amy thought, suddenly angry at that possibility. After all, she kept no secrets from her mother, she thought. No big secrets at least. Except that she hated ballet and dance class and she didn't like piano and sometimes she wanted to throw her ice skates away. It was true that she had never told her mother anything that might hurt her feelings.

The Halloween parade would be starting soon. Amy checked her watch: 1:45. Just now, if she were at Barton School, she would be in the bathroom with the girls in her class who had decided to be in the parade this year, changing into her Queen of Hearts costume. Soon they would line up in the corridor outside the auditorium. Ms. Ploy would be playing the piano—probably "Puff the Magic Dragon," which was Ms. Ploy's favorite, and the younger children, delirious with happiness, the older children, giggling, slightly embarrassed in their disguises, would be marching down the aisle of the auditorium, one by one across the stage in front of the judges. Usually Amy won the Grand Prize for the best costume—four out of her seven years at Barton. And she did feel wistful that she had not gone to school. But she was pleased as well. The day had gone by easily. She had been alone in New York City among strangers. She had faced danger at Washington Square and survived. She had eaten exactly the kind of lunch she had wanted to eat. For the first time ever, she had been in charge of her own life.

At Macy's, she stopped to look for a birthday present for Camilla, who collected china horses, and found a high-stepping palomino about the size of an orange juice glass that Camilla would love. But the price on the bottom said forty-eight dollars. She found a picture frame for seven dollars for her mother for Christmas—a small, oblong picture frame with tiny yellow roses in which she could put her school picture, which had been better than usual this year. She felt entirely grown up, standing in line with the customers at Macy's, giving the salesperson a ten-dollar bill. Then she walked briskly along Fifth Avenue to FAO Schwartz Toy Store. For a long time, she wandered from aisle to aisle through the toys, although she was almost too old for toys. The sleds for Christmas were already on display, although there was no sledding to be had in New York City. But Amy remembered one wonderful weekend at Camilla's country house in Connecticut, sledding down the hill in back of the house, across the frozen pond.

That evening, going home on the train with her mother, she had asked Nicole—without thinking or she would not have brought up the subject of fathers—but she asked her, "If I had a father, might we have a country house?"

Nicole had lost her temper. "It has nothing to do with fathers," she said. "I give you lessons so you'll have a full life to make up for the fact we live in the city, Amy," she had said. "So you will know how to do the things country children do. Like ice-skating. You ice-skated as well as Camilla," she had said. "Even better."

The saleswoman in bicycles asked, did Amy want to try a bike?

"No, thank you," Amy said. "I'm just looking today."

"No school today?" the nosy saleswoman asked.

"I don't go to school, yet," Amy said quickly. "I just moved to New York from Alaska."

"Alaska?" the salesperson said, interested in this information. "Where in Alaska?" she asked.

Amy couldn't for the moment think of any

place in Alaska although later, after she had left FAO Schwartz, she remembered Anchorage.

"Oh, all over Alaska," she replied.

Just in a single day, not even eight hours, she had gotten quite good at lying.

The crosstown bus was full of schoolchildren with their backpacks over one shoulder, chattering back and forth, and Amy was suddenly lonely. She wondered what Molly talked about to Camilla during recess, and whether Terry and Sally had made up after their fight at Molly's sleepover, and whether she'd gotten a good grade in her social studies test on Tuesday, and whether she would have played goalie in soccer today. She wondered who had won the Grand Prize in the Halloween parade. It was only three-thirty. She'd have to wait for two hours before Molly got home from soccer to know what she had missed. She opened the backpack and took out the box with the frame she had gotten for her mother. Maybe she wouldn't put her school picture in the frame, she thought. Maybe instead, she'd put the picture she had found of her father that morning and hidden in her sweater drawer: *Love of my Life, Forever, Peter.*

And then she remembered the man she'd seen outside the Austin Grille with her mother. He had been too far away for her to recognize him, if she knew him at all. Perhaps he was a lawyer from another law firm. Or a client.

She got off the bus and crossed the street.

Inside, the apartment smelled musty, and she opened the window that overlooked a tiny sliver of the Hudson River. She turned on the radio to all music and checked the answering machine. There were four messages. The first was from Molly Loeb. "Hello, Amy. Where are you? I'm calling from school with Camilla, and we just had recess and guess what, Billy Tonkins was hit by a car yesterday but he's okay. Where are you? Are you watching TV? Please answer." The second caller hung up. The third was from Mme. Periot, calling to say she had meant to call Mme. Dunn at zee office, and the fourth call was the Metropolitan Opera, asking for subscriptions. Amy erased the calls. She went into the kitchen and opened

the refrigerator. A small chicken was de-
frosting on the first shelf. There was a bowl of
green grapes, leftover tuna salad, Pepperidge
Farm whole-wheat bread, a bunch of celery,
some cut-up carrots, margarine, two eggs,
plum jelly. Only pasta and a pork roast in the
freezer. No ice cream. No cookies. No graham
crackers. No Triskets even. Only the dry,
white, rice cakes Nicole ate for snacks to keep
from gaining weight.

Boring, Amy thought and left the kitchen,
wandering through the living room, into her
mother's bedroom and then into her own. She
took out the frame she had gotten at Macy's
and put the picture of her father in it. He
looked very cheerful and handsome surrounded with yellow roses. She put the frame
with the picture on her dresser. It was four-
thirty. She sat down at the end of her bed. A
whole hour, maybe more, before Molly was
home from school, and time was crawling very
slowly.

She took off her mother's skirt and sweater
and hung them up in the closet. Then she
tried on the Queen of Hearts costume. It was
a very pretty costume, with a bright red top

with small red hearts around the neckline and a white satin skirt. But in the long mirror on her mother's door, the costume made Amy look fat, as if her hips were broad as a piano.

She sat down at her mother's desk and typed, "Please excuse Amy Dunn's absence on October 31, 1993. She had the flu." *Nicole Dunn,* she signed in blue ink. She folded up the note and put it in her backpack.

Molly would be home at five-thirty, and they'd go trick-or-treating then, before Nicole got home from the office at seven-thirty, before dinner. Maybe Camilla could come with them or Beatrice Tree, who lived in the apartment next door.

Amy turned on the television and lay down on the couch, her head resting against the puffed sleeves of the Queen of Hearts dress, and in seconds, she had fallen sound asleep.

CHAPTER 10

Mr. Rappaport was just entering the apartment building when the taxi with Nicole Dunn stopped at 495 West End Avenue, and he held the door for her.

"Home early?" he asked, following her into the elevator.

"A little," Nicole said, weak with worry about Amy. She pushed the up button on the elevator.

"Well, I spent the day with an old high school friend," Mr. Rappaport said. "She recognized me on the subway after all these years."

"That was nice for you," Nicole said absently.

"I almost spent the day with your daughter

until my high school friend turned up on the subway."

"Amy?"

"The very same," Mr. Rappaport said cheerfully. "I had nothing to do today, and it was too beautiful to stay indoors, so I was going with her to the dentist."

"With Amy to the dentist?"

"She was on her way to the dentist, and I thought why not? I'll just go to the dentist with Amy Dunn since I have nothing better to do, and then we'll get a chocolate shake or a Coke, and I'll walk her back to school."

"I see," Nicole said. Although she did not see at all. Had Amy gotten a sudden toothache after Nicole left for work? Had she pretended to Guy Rappaport that she was going to the dentist? *Please hurry to the ninth floor*, she wished the slow-moving elevator. But what if when she arrived in Apartment 9B, Amy wasn't there? Then what? She was so worried, she could hardly breathe.

"It was nice to see you, Nicole," Mr. Rappaport was saying.

"Nice to see you too, Guy," Nicole said, and with shaking hands, she opened the door to

Apartment 9B, arriving just as the telephone stopped ringing and the voice of Molly Loeb was on the answering machine.

"Hiya, Amy," Molly said. "I'm at soccer practice, using the pay phone, but the weirdest thing is I saw your mother at the Halloween parade like she didn't even know you were sick. I'll call you when I get home. Bye bye bye bye bye."

Amy, half sleeping in front of the television, jumped up when she heard Molly's voice.

But when she turned around, there was her mother, standing in the doorway.

Amy slid back into the couch. "Oh, brother."

"Amy," Nicole said thinly. "What is going on?"

"What is going on?" Amy asked slowly, stalling for time. "Well, I don't exactly know," she began.

Until today, Amy Dunn had only lied once, and that to her mother in the third grade when she lost her math book and didn't know the answers on her math test, but this Halloween afternoon, she was stuck. "I'm sick," she said.

"Sick?" Nicole asked.

Amy nodded.

"You weren't sick this morning when I left for work."

"I was," Amy said. "I didn't want to trouble you because you had a trial this morning."

Nicole sat down in the chair across from Amy and crossed her legs, hesitating before she spoke again.

"I went to school because it was your last Halloween parade," Nicole said.

"I know," Amy said gloomily. "I heard Molly on the answering machine."

"Why didn't you call my office and tell Victoria you were sick?"

"I'm really sorry," Amy said. "I should have."

"And then just now on the elevator I saw Mr. Rappaport."

Oh, brother, Amy thought.

"And he said you had gone to the dentist today," Nicole said. "Was your sickness a toothache?"

"No," Amy said. "Excuse me," and she ran to the bathroom, slamming the door behind her. "I think I'm going to throw up," she called through the door. In the bathroom mirror, she looked chalk white, but she was not going to be sick, she supposed, unless her sudden troubles were making her sick. She wanted to fly out the window of the bathroom, fly over Manhattan, and not come back until Thanksgiving when her mother would be so glad to see her, she'd forgive her for Halloween.

"Amy?" Nicole called. "Are you okay?"

"Not really," Amy said, leaning against the bathroom door, wondering what next to do. Maybe she could spend the night in the bathroom.

"Do you need my help?" Nicole asked.

"No," Amy said, washing her face to get rid of the makeup from the morning. When she turned off the spigot, she listened at the door and heard nothing. Her mother was probably standing right in the hall in front of the bathroom door. Soon, Amy knew, she was simply going to have to open the door and tell her mother the truth.

Nicole was leaning against the wall in front of her, her arms folded across her chest, when Amy came out.

"Do you want a cup of tea?" she asked Amy.

"Yes, please," Amy said, following her mother into the kitchen.

"So, tell me what happened today?" Nicole asked, turning the fire on under the kettle.

"Okay," Amy said, her stomach fluttering with butterflies. She took two teacups down from the cupboard and sat at the kitchen table.

"This morning when I woke up," she began. "I saw the dress you had made for me for Halloween." She put her head in her hands to avoid her mother's eyes. "And I felt awful."

"Awful?" Nicole asked. "You mean sick?"

"Not regular sick," Amy said. "Heartsick."

She did not have to tell her mother the truth, she thought. She could tell her half a truth about the Halloween parade. But she went on anyway.

"I didn't want to be in the Halloween parade. I really didn't want to be in it," Amy said. "And then I felt terrible because you had made my costume as usual, and, as usual, it was beautiful."

"I was afraid of that," Nicole said. "You did tell me in September that you didn't really want a costume this year. And then the next day, you changed your mind. I should have paid more attention." She poured tea, took out milk and sugar, and sat down at the kitchen table across from Amy.

"I didn't want to hurt your feelings," Amy said, putting more sugar in her tea.

"I wish you had told me," Nicole said quietly.

"It was more than the Halloween parade," Amy said, and she could feel her throat filling, as if the words were drowning her. "It's everything. I don't want to take ballet lessons because I'm terrible. And I don't want to take piano lessons or French lessons," she said, her eyes filling with tears. "I don't want to be a goalie in soccer or have to get the highest grades in the class every single time. I woke up this morning and I wanted to quit."

"Oh, Amy," Nicole said. "I didn't know. I honestly didn't know. I thought you liked to be so busy."

"I hate it," Amy said.

"You should have told me," Nicole said.

"I was afraid to tell you," Amy said. "I was

afraid to hurt your feelings. But this morning when I woke up it was too much, and I decided to go on vacation."

"From everything?"

"Everything. I called Mme. Periot."

"That explains why Mme. Periot hoped you would be feeling better."

"What she really hopes is that I quit ballet so that my floppy stomach doesn't ruin her stupid *Nutcracker*," Amy said. "I wish we had some cookies."

"We don't," Nicole said.

"I know. I looked everywhere."

Nicole opened her purse beside the kitchen table, took out a Milky Way, and cut it in half.

"I didn't think you ate candy bars," Amy said.

"At work," Nicole said, handing Amy her half. "When I'm tired, I eat candy bars. So what about piano?"

"Mr. Barnes sits in the chair behind me and falls asleep while I play the piano."

"He does?"

"Like this," Amy said, sitting on the edge of her chair with her eyes closed, wobbling to and fro. "Now, Amy," she mumbled, imitating

Mr. Barnes. "Play that charming little tune again."

Nicole was smiling.

"I'm terrible at piano."

"And did you cancel ballet class?"

Amy nodded.

Nicole folded her arms on the table and leaned toward Amy.

"And you cancelled school?"

Amy nodded. "I told Ms. Applewood that you would write a note tomorrow," Amy said, hardly able to believe herself, sitting in her own kitchen, speaking the unspeakable truth to her mother. "So I wrote the note and signed it, copying your signature from one of your checks."

Nicole had started to laugh. The laughter began slowly like a giggle and spread across her face and in her throat until she was laughing so hard, tears were pouring down her cheeks, and she had to stand up.

"And then," Amy began quickly, astonished at her mother's high good humor.

"And then you probably went to Washington Square on the subway," Nicole said, catching her breath.

"How did you know, Mommy?" Amy asked.

Nicole reached over and pulled Amy on her lap.

"I guessed. I just guessed because that's what I would have done if I were you," Nicole said. "You have been too good for too long."

"And you have been trying so hard to do the best thing," Amy said, leaning against her mother's shoulder.

"That's right," said Nicole. She settled back into the chair. "So you were not really sick just now?" Nicole asked.

"I was nervous to tell you the truth," Amy said. "That made me feel sick."

"I know that feeling," Nicole said, "because I have it right now."

"You do?" Amy asked.

"I do." Nicole rested her chin in her hands. "We have been keeping secrets from each other."

"I already know what happened to you," Amy said, getting up and pouring another cup of tea. "A man kissed you in front of the Austin Grille."

Nicole's stomach fell.

"I saw," Amy said. "When I was walking

home from Washington Square. Are you going to marry him?"

"No, no, of course not," Nicole said, straightening her skirt, flushed with embarrassment that Amy had seen her. "He is a friend with whom I have lunch," she began. "And I like him very much, but I have never brought him home because I was afraid to hurt your feelings."

"Why would it hurt my feelings?" Amy asked.

"It just felt to me as if it might upset you," Nicole said, "because I'm all you have."

"Oh, no, Mommy, I have plenty of people like Molly and Camilla and Beatrice," Amy said. "It's you who have only me."

The telephone rang, and it was Molly Loeb.

"Just a moment, Molly," Nicole said. She put her hand over the receiver. "Molly would like you to go trick-or-treating," Nicole said. "But maybe afterward you'd like to go out with me."

"Let's go out now," Amy said. "I was too sick today for trick or treating."

Nicole laughed and told Molly no, but Amy would be back in school tomorrow.

Nicole sat down at the kitchen table.

"What is your favorite thing of all the things we do in New York City?" she asked.

"What do you think?" Amy laughed. "You ought to know."

"Dinner at the Austin Grille."

"Exactly," Amy said.

"Mine too," Nicole said. "So change and let's go."

Amy hung up her costume, changed to her dark-green corduroy jumper and a turtleneck, brushed her short hair, and followed Nicole out of the apartment.

At Eighty-fifth they hailed a cab downtown, and Amy settled in the backseat, next to her mother.

"It's funny," Amy said softly, letting her head rest against her mother. "We were thinking the same thing and didn't know it."

The darkness fell between them and when she looked, Amy could only see the outline of her mother's face and, through the window, the skyline of New York City, spray painted with dancing lights.